978-1-938700-28-6

Published by Commonwealth Editions, an imprint of Applewood Books, Inc.,
Box 27, Carlisle, Massachusetts 01741

Visit us on the web at www.commonwealtheditions.com
Visit Shankman and O'Neill on the web at www.shankmanoneill.com

Printed in China

10 9 8 7 6 5 4 3 2 1

WHEN a LOBSTER BUYS a BATHROBE

by ED SHANKMAN • illustrated by DAVE O'NEILL

Commonwealth Editions
Carlisle, Massachusetts

WHEN A LOBSTER SEES A PUPPET SHOW,

he stays until the end.
He watches by himself sometimes,
or he may bring a friend.

To make sure he hears every word,
the lobster's very quiet.
That's not the case with everyone
(but others ought to try it).

WHEN A LOBSTER EATS A RAISIN,
he delights in every bite.
And that is quite important
'cause he bites one every night.

Once he's chewed the whole thing up,
it settles in his tummy.
And sometimes he has seconds
'cause the first one was so yummy!

WHEN A LOBSTER PLAYS WITH MONKEYS,
he does just what monkeys do.
He swings around from tree to tree and eats bananas too.
The monkeys never think he's unlike them in any way.
(Or perhaps they really do and they're just too polite to say.)

WHEN A LOBSTER RIDES A MOTORBIKE,
he leans into the breeze.
He rides in perfect balance, taking every curve with ease.
He keeps his focus straight ahead and never looks behind.
If something happens way back there, the lobster doesn't mind.

WHEN A LOBSTER KNITS A SCARF,

he uses very special yarn.
He gets it from a sheep he knows who lives out in the barn.
When, at last, the scarf is done and stunning to behold,
The lobster gives it to the sheep so she won't catch a cold.

WHEN A LOBSTER PLANTS A MARIGOLD,

he places it just so.
It seems he knows exactly what will make that flower grow.
He gives the seed a magic mix of water, love, and sun.
And that's the kind of gardening that cannot be outdone!

When a lobster packs a suitcase,

every item has its place.
Between the seams he packs some creams to moisturize his face.
He probably won't use them but he packs them just in case.
(It really doesn't matter 'cause they don't take up much space.)

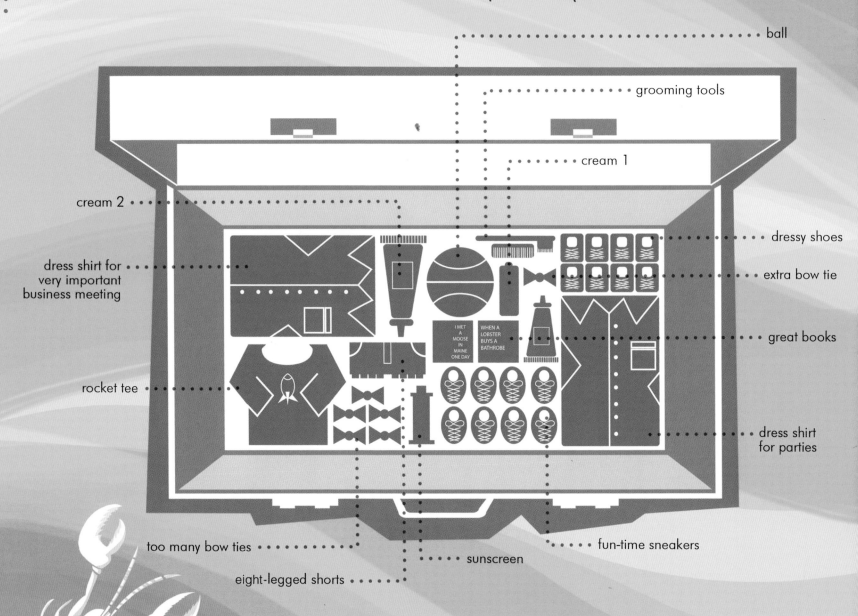

ball

grooming tools

cream 1

cream 2

dressy shoes

dress shirt for very important business meeting

extra bow tie

great books

rocket tee

dress shirt for parties

too many bow ties

sunscreen

eight-legged shorts

fun-time sneakers

WHEN A LOBSTER TAKES A PHOTOGRAPH,

he chooses what he shoots.

He may not shoot a centipede unless he's wearing boots.

Or maybe he wears saddle shoes, or something in a slipper.

Or something with a buckle, or a button, or a zipper.

WHEN A LOBSTER BUYS A BATHROBE,
he makes sure to take his time.
If the fabric isn't thick and soft, he will not spend a dime.
He knows exactly what he wants, and only wants the best.

And if he doesn't find it, he prefers to go undressed!

WHEN A LOBSTER WEARS A PARACHUTE,

he floats across the sky.
He watches eagles ride the wind and sees the clouds go by.
With nothing else to do up there and no one else around,
He likes to dream of all the things he'll do back on the ground.

WHEN A LOBSTER DRINKS A MILKSHAKE,

he prefers to use a straw.
He places it precisely, then he holds it with his claw.
He drinks the potion, sip by sip, while tasting every taste.
And by the time he's finished, not a droplet goes to waste.

WHEN A LOBSTER PAINTS A MASTERPIECE,

he always signs his name.
But the painting's not complete until he puts it in a frame.
Finally he hangs it, making certain that it's straight.
And that's the way a master makes a masterpiece look great.

Lobster (2015)
oil on canvas
by Lobster

WHEN A LOBSTER MEETS A UNICORN,

he always shows respect.
There are simply no exceptions. (And, believe me, I have checked.)
That's just the way these lobsters are, according to my source.
And then, of course, a unicorn's no ordinary horse.

... but shorter pants means there's a chance he plans on playing sports.

WOOOOOO OOOOOW

WHEN A LOBSTER SEES A RAINBOW,

he can't seem to look away.
The beauty stops him in his tracks, and that's where he will stay.

Unless that rainbow disappears, the lobster stays all day.
And if he misses something else, that's perfectly okay.

NÄR EN HUMMER STUDERAR SVENSKA, *

*TRANSLATION: **WHEN A LOBSTER STUDIES SWEDISH,**

he remembers every word.
Which is why he feels at home wherever Swedish words are heard.

He's also known to hold his own in Latin and in Greek.
While pigs speak Latin too, whatever Greek they speak is weak.

WHEN A LOBSTER SINGS THE BLUES,

he puts his soul in every note.
The same cannot be said of a coyote or a goat.

They simply do not share the lobster's flair for melody.

(Though a goat may dance a little
if he thinks no one will see.)

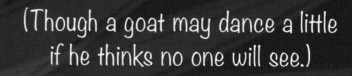

WHEN A LOBSTER MEETS A MOVIE STAR,
he doesn't stop and stare.
He just keeps right on walking as if nobody is there.
'Cause fame is simply not enough to catch a lobster's eye.
But he will stop if he sees something funny passing by.

WHEN A LOBSTER RIDES A SEESAW,
he goes up or he goes down.
When he's sitting way up top,
he has a perfect view of town.

When he's sitting on the bottom he looks up into the sky.

And when he's in between he watches people passing by.

WHEN A LOBSTER AND A TSETSE FLY SPEND TOO MUCH TIME INSIDE,

They may get on each other's nerves and both may want to hide.
They may pretend they're busy paying bills or doing chores.

But in the end they're fine
if they just spend some time outdoors.

WHEN A LOBSTER WRITES A CHILDREN'S BOOK,
he measures every word.
He has a knack for rhyming (or, at least that's what I've heard).

WHEN A LOBSTER DRINKS A MILKSHAKE,
he prefers to use a straw.
He places it precisely. Then he holds it with his claw.
He drinks the potion, sip by sip, while tasting every taste.
And by the time he's finished, not a droplet goes to waste.

You might think he'd write about a wizard or an elf.
But typically, as you can see, he writes about himself.

WHEN A LOBSTER'S WITH HIS CLOSEST FRIENDS,
he plays the day away.
For there's no greater joy in life than lobster friends at play.
And if they're in the ocean, well, that's even better yet.
'Cause everything a lobster loves is better when it's wet!

So if you're in the ocean
and you hear the sound of laughter,

HAHAHAHAHA!

HAHAHAHA!

You'll know you've found our lobster living happily ever after.

The End!

WHEN A LOBSTER _____

_____

_____

_____

_____

WHAT ELSE DOES A LOBSTER DO?
Create your own rhyme
and draw a picture to go with it!

ALSO by Ed Shankman and Dave O'Neill

My Grandma Lives in Florida
The Boston Balloonies
The Cods of Cape Cod
I Met a Moose in Maine One Day
Champ and Me by the Maple Tree
The Bourbon Street Band is Back

Also by Ed Shankman with Dave Frank

I Went to the Party in Kalamazoo

Ed Shankman

Ed's entire life has been one continuous creative project. In addition to writing, playing music, and painting, he is the chief creative officer at an advertising agency, where he helps others discover and focus their own creative voices. As you can see by this book, Ed fancies himself the world's leading expert on the imaginary lives of lobsters. He lives in Verona, NJ, with his wife, Miriam.

Dave O'Neill

Dave has worked as a graphic designer and illustrator since graduating from art school. When he's not illustrating children's books, he is an art director specializing in advertising and marketing, a toy designer, and an improvisational comedian. Dave would like you to believe that he traveled the world documenting the habits and hobbies of lobsters, but he probably did not. Or did he? Hard to say. Dave spends his days as a husband and father to the two prettiest girls he knows.